D1208943

DEDICATION

To the kids that never give up, and keep us laughing every day.

All inquires about this book can be sent to the publisher at: BannonRiverBooks@gmail.com

Published in the United States by Bannon River Books, LLC

ISBN: 978-0-9908842-5-5

For more information, or to book an in-person or virtual event visit: www.ColleenBrunetti.com

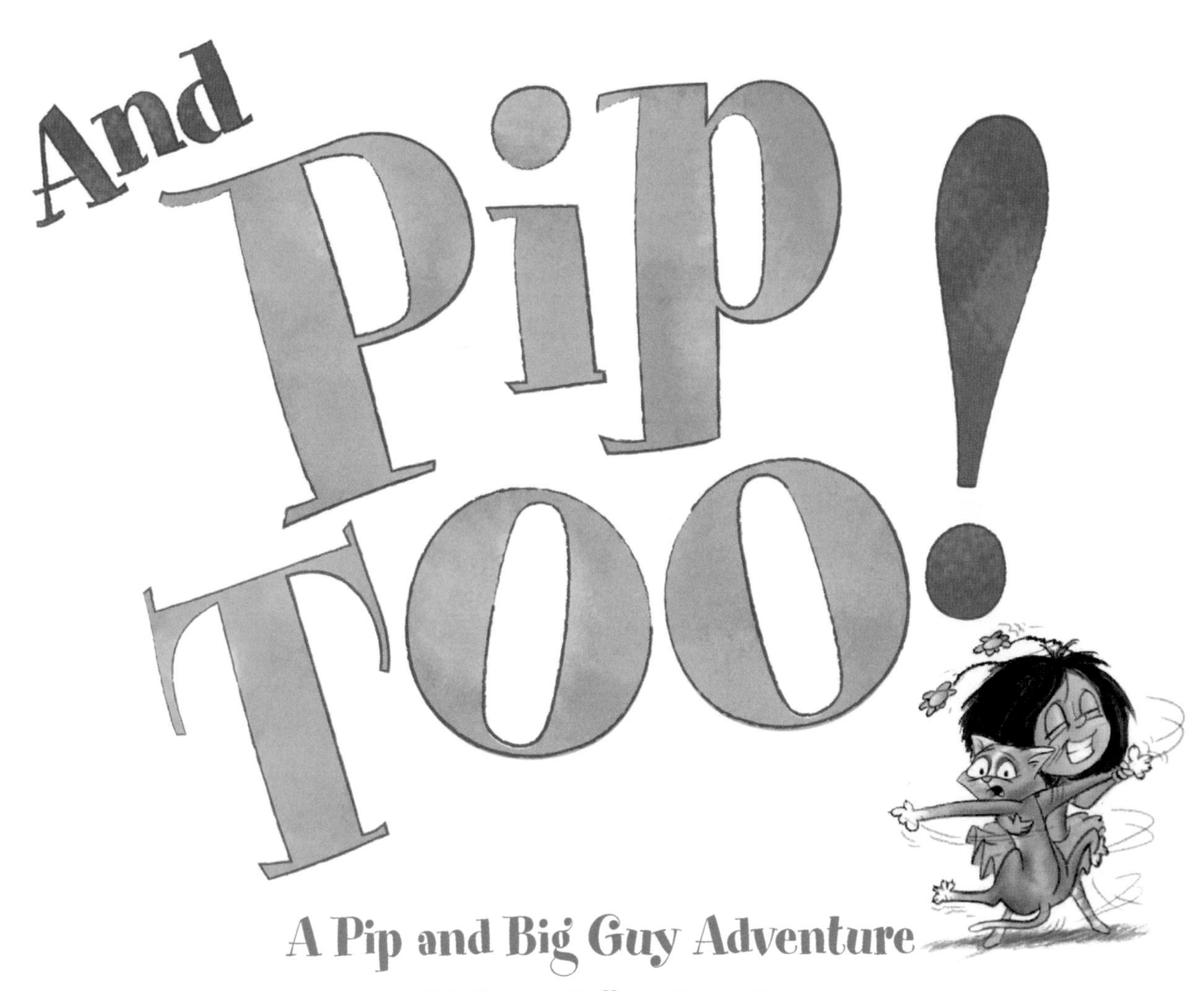

Written by Colleen Brunetti

Illustrated by Dan Carsten

Big Guy woke up bright and early.

He stretched his toes

with a

yawn.

What had woken him from
such sweet dreams,
just a few minutes
before
dawn?

SHE WAS UP!
Pip!
It was about
to begin.
He knew it was
sure to start.

Big Guy jumped from his bed,

a pitter-patter

in his heart.

They slid downstairs
in footed jammies,
smelling
something
good.

Then **Pip**

began to do her thing,
as only this Pip could.

He ate his scrambled eggs
and toast and
some potato hash.

"ME TOO!" said Pip
as she opened the milk
and poured it with a
Splash.

He next built a wooden tower so very tall and red.

"ME TOO!" said Pip as she placed one block and it crashed

down

upon his head.

He went outside
to get some air
and try to
ride his bike.

"ME TOO!" said Pip as she startled the cat with her zippy, purple trike.

He tried at last
to stop and rest
beneath the
big oak tree.

"ME TOO!" said Pip
as she placed a
fuzzy
spider
on his knee.

He came inside to take a breath and maybe read a while.

"ME TOO!" said Pip as she covered his lap with a gigantic board book pile.

He donned
his pirate costume
next, a hat upon
his head.

"ME TOO!" said Pip
as she swapped it for
a princess crown instead.

He got his recorder
and tried to play

just a
little tune.

"ME TOO!" said Pip
as she played on his head
with a wooden spoon.

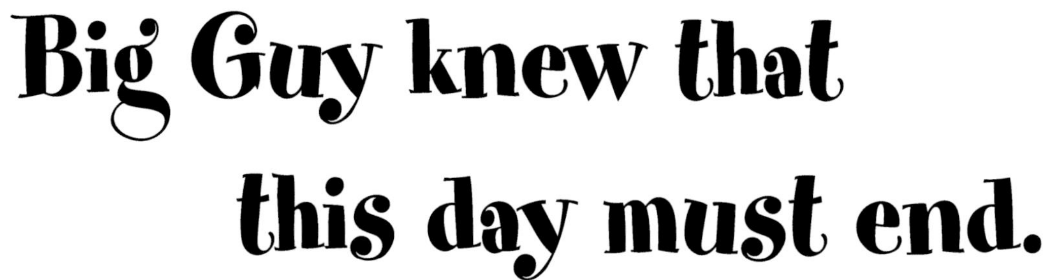

Big Guy knew that
this day must end.

It was
DEFINITELY
time for bed.

His only hope was
a song and a kiss.
Maybe then she'd
rest her head.

"That's it!" he said. "I'm so
exhausted, can't you plainly see?"
Then little Pip was suddenly
sweet as only
she could be.

She let out a squeal and giggle,
followed by a yawn.
Pip grabbed her blanket
and her bear;
the **wiggles**
were all gone.

There in the evening glow,
the moon and stars
all shining bright,

Big Guy said,
"It's been
quite a day,
but I guess
that you're
all right."

"YOU TOO!" said Pip,
as she snuggled in tight.
"I love you big brother,

Good night ... Good night."

COMING SOON!

"To The Zoo With You!"

A Pip And Big Guy Adventure: Book Two

Sign up to be notified about our upcoming books!
https://www.colleenbrunetti.com/pip-and-big-guy

Please consider leaving an Amazon or Good Reads review. They really help!

Thank you!

Colleen Brunetti grew up in the rolling green hills of Vermont, where she spent much of her time devouring books. That love of literacy led to a career in teaching, and later to becoming an author. Today she spends her time with her husband, chasing their two kids and multiple pets, and dreaming up her next publications.
Learn more at www.ColleenBrunetti.com

For as long as he can remember, Dan knew he wanted to be an artist. Influenced by Saturday morning cartoons, he would spend hours drawing the silly stories and characters of his imagination. Today, Dan continues to bring stories and characters of all kinds to life but he has traded in his crayons and markers for paintbrushes and a graphics tablet. When not sketching and painting, Dan enjoys spending time with his wife, playing with their two boys, and watching the Boston Red Sox.
Follow Dan's work on Facebook or Instagram: @DanCarstenIllustration

Made in the
USA
Monee, IL

15402371R10021